Eclipse Reaver

The Eclipse Chronicles, Volume 2

Kenneth Thomas

Published by Kenneth Thomas, 2024.

ECLIPSE REAVER

First edition. November 17, 2024.

ISBN: 979-8230185307

Written by Kenneth Thomas.

Also by Kenneth Thomas

The Awakening Thread Chronicles
The Awakening Thread

The Convergence of Minds series
The Digital Agora: A Philosophical Epic of AI and Humanity
Foundation of the Agora
Beyond the Agora: Fractured Realms

The Eclipse Chronicles
Shards of Light
Eclipse Reaver

The Veil of Shadows Series
Shattered Dominion
The Fractured Path

Standalone

A Tail of Darkness To Light

The Mirror Within

Echoes of Ink and Heart

Purpose Over Power: The Visionary Path of Servant Leadership

The Questions That Shape Us: Finding Life's Wisdom-The Power of Inquiry

Where the Shadows Settle

30 Days to Inner Freedom: A Mindful Journey in Addiction Recovery

Towards a Sustainable Future: The UN's 17 Goals

Echoes of Becoming

Eclipse Reaver
The Eclipse Chronicles
By Kenneth Thomas

PROLOGUE: THE SHATTERED Path

The cavern walls whispered with fractured echoes, carrying the faint sounds of footsteps through the ancient, shadow-drenched corridors. The remnants of the shard pulsed faintly in Cyrix's hand, a fractured fragment of the Axis's power that burned cold against his palm. Its light - neither wholly bright nor truly dark - cast flickering shadows that danced like specters around him.

He moved with purpose through the ruins of the Umbral Depths, his cloak trailing behind him like a specter's shroud. Each step carried him deeper into the forgotten heart of the shadowed realm, where the air grew heavier, alive with the residue of ancient power.

The shards were gone, reclaimed by the Axis and used to forge the Eclipse. But the echoes of their influence still lingered, scattered across Ecliptica like scars on the world's surface. Cyrix's fragmented shard was proof of that - a jagged remnant that refused to fade, tethering him to the power he had sought to control.

"They think it's over," Cyrix murmured, his voice low, reverent. "They think the Axis is whole."

The shard pulsed, its faint glow illuminating the intricate carvings on the cavern walls. Symbols of light and shadow entwined in perfect harmony, their patterns spiraling toward a central image: a figure standing between two celestial orbs, one of blinding light and the other of infinite darkness.

Cyrix paused, his gaze fixed on the carving. His fingers brushed the shard, its resonance vibrating faintly against his skin.

"They don't understand," he said, his voice growing sharper. "Balance is nothing more than the calm before collapse. True unity demands something stronger. Something absolute."

He pressed his hand against the wall, the shard's energy surging through him. The symbols pulsed in response, their patterns unraveling as the air around him crackled with power. The ground beneath his feet trembled, and a low rumble echoed through the cavern.

A voice, ancient and guttural, filled the space. "What do you seek, shard-bearer?"

Cyrix straightened, his eyes glowing faintly with the shard's fractured light. "Power. Purpose. The strength to reshape this world into what it was always meant to be."

The voice laughed, a deep, resonant sound that reverberated through the cavern. "You seek control. Yet you stand before chaos."

Cyrix's expression hardened. "Chaos is a tool, not a master. And I will wield it to forge a world where the Eclipse is more than a symbol - it is an empire."

The ground trembled again, and a dark fissure split open at the center of the chamber. From its depths, a surge of shadow and light erupted, swirling together in a chaotic dance. Cyrix stepped forward, his shard pulsing in time with the energy.

"I will become the Eclipse Reaver," he said, his voice steady, unwavering. "And I will bring this world to its knees."

The energy surged around him, swallowing him in its chaotic embrace. The light of the shard flared, its fractured glow spreading through the cavern as the symbols on the walls disintegrated into shadow.

And then there was silence.

Chapter One: Whispers in the Twilight

The Eclipse hung low in the sky, its light a soft blend of violet and gold that bathed the Twilight Marches in its serene glow. But Kaelion Ashtear knew better than to trust serenity. The world had been quiet since the Axis was reforged, but the scars left behind by the shards lingered, faint tremors in the fabric of Ecliptica.

He tightened his grip on the hilt of his sword as he stepped into the outskirts of a Twilight encampment. The grass beneath his boots glimmered faintly with stardust, its silvery sheen broken by the heavy tread of many feet. The air carried a subtle tension, the kind that settled just before a storm.

Selara walked a few paces ahead, her movements smooth and deliberate. She no longer wore the shadows that had once coiled around her like a second skin, but her presence carried the same quiet intensity.

"You're sure about this?" Kaelion asked, his voice low.

Selara glanced back at him, her violet eyes catching the Eclipse's glow. "Not even a little. But if we don't stop this now, we're going to have much bigger problems."

Kaelion frowned. They'd heard the rumors: a rising force in the Umbral Depths, led by someone calling themselves the Reaver. The stories varied - some claimed it was Cyrix, back from the dead; others spoke of a shadow-born warlord wielding the shards' corrupted remnants. Whatever the truth, it was enough to pull them back into the fray.

The closer they got, the more the air seemed to hum with an unnatural resonance, faint but unmistakable. Kaelion knew that sensation all too well.

"The shards," he muttered.

Selara nodded. "Something's feeding off them. Or what's left of them."

The encampment came into view, a cluster of makeshift tents and smoldering fires scattered across the rolling hills. Twilight clans had gathered here, their banners marked with symbols of shadowlight - blending the traditions of the Umbral Depths and Solaris Citadel.

But it wasn't unity that had brought them together.

Kaelion scanned the encampment, his eyes narrowing at the sight of armed guards patrolling the perimeter. Their armor was piecemeal, scavenged from battles long past, but their weapons glinted with a dark, unnatural energy.

Selara crouched beside him, her gaze sharp. "That's not ordinary steel."

"No," Kaelion agreed. "It's shard-forged."

The guards' weapons carried the faint, chaotic glow of shards - remnants of the Axis's fractured power, twisted and reshaped into tools of war.

"They're arming themselves for something big," Kaelion said.

"Or someone big," Selara replied.

Before they could move closer, a shadow fell across them. Kaelion's hand went to his sword, but Selara raised a hand to stop him.

"Wait," she said, her voice low.

The figure stepped into the light, revealing an older man with a weathered face and sharp, calculating eyes. His cloak bore the markings of the Silverveil clan, but his posture carried an air of authority that set him apart from the others.

"You shouldn't be here," the man said, his tone calm but firm.

Kaelion straightened, his expression guarded. "Neither should half the people in that camp."

The man's eyes flicked between them, lingering on Selara. "You're the shadow-sculptor. The one who helped restore the Axis."

Selara's jaw tightened, but she said nothing.

"And you," the man continued, turning to Kaelion, "the knight who fell from grace."

Kaelion's grip on his sword tightened. "We didn't come here to talk about the past. We came to stop whatever's happening here."

The man's gaze darkened. "You think you can stop this? You don't even know what you're dealing with."

"Then why don't you enlighten us?" Selara said, her tone sharp.

The man hesitated, his shoulders stiffening. "The Reaver isn't just a warlord. He's... something else. Something born of the shards' corruption."

Kaelion exchanged a glance with Selara. "Cyrix?"

The man shook his head. "No. Worse."

The sound of a horn cut through the air, its low, mournful tone sending a shiver down Kaelion's spine. The encampment stirred, guards snapping to attention as the gathered clans turned toward the source of the sound.

Kaelion followed their gaze to the far side of the camp, where a figure emerged from the shadows.

The Reaver.

The figure was clad in jagged armor that pulsed with faint light and shadow, its edges sharp and unnatural. The air around him seemed to ripple, as though the world itself recoiled from his presence.

Kaelion's chest tightened. The energy emanating from the Reaver was unlike anything he'd felt before - chaotic, relentless, and deeply wrong.

Selara's voice was barely above a whisper. "What is that?"

The man beside them didn't answer. His expression was grim, his eyes fixed on the Reaver as the figure raised a hand, his voice booming across the camp.

"The shards were only the beginning," the Reaver said, his tone resonating with power. "The Axis has been reforged, but it is incomplete. This world will not survive its own fragility. Only through strength can we ensure its future. Only through power can we bring true unity!"

The gathered clans erupted in cheers, their voices a chaotic chorus that sent chills through Kaelion.

Selara's jaw tightened. "He's building an army."

"And he's not going to stop here," Kaelion said.

The Reaver's gaze swept across the encampment, and for a moment, his glowing eyes locked onto Kaelion and Selara's hiding spot.

Kaelion's breath caught. The Reaver smiled, a sharp, predatory expression.

"Let them come," he said.

Chapter Two: Shadows Rising

The camp was in chaos. The Reaver's presence had ignited a fervor that rippled through the gathered clans like a wildfire. Shouts and cheers echoed across the hills as warriors prepared for battle, sharpening their shard-forged weapons and hoisting banners marked with symbols of shadow and light.

Kaelion and Selara crouched in the underbrush, their gazes locked on the Reaver as he moved through the camp. His armor gleamed with a dark, unnatural energy, and the air around him seemed to pulse with a rhythm that Kaelion could feel in his bones.

"That's not just shard energy," Kaelion whispered. "It's something else."

Selara's eyes narrowed. "It feels like the Axis, but... corrupted. Twisted."

The man from the Silverveil clan, who had introduced himself as Darith, knelt beside them, his expression grim. "The Reaver's power comes from the remnants of the shards, but it's more than that. He's found something deeper. Something ancient."

Kaelion frowned. "And you're just letting him build an army under your nose?"

Darith's jaw tightened. "You think we haven't tried to stop him? He's not just a man. He's... an idea. And ideas are harder to kill than people."

A commotion in the camp drew their attention. A group of warriors stood in a circle, their voices raised in anger as they argued over provisions. The tension escalated quickly, and in an instant, one of the warriors drew his weapon, its shard-forged edge gleaming dangerously.

Before anyone could intervene, the Reaver stepped forward.

The air grew heavy, and the warriors froze, their weapons faltering. The Reaver raised a hand, his voice calm but commanding.

"There is no room for division," he said, his tone resonating with an unnatural authority. "We fight as one, or we fall apart."

The warriors lowered their weapons, their heads bowed in submission. The Reaver turned away, his presence leaving a palpable silence in its wake.

Selara exhaled slowly. "He's not just using fear. He's controlling them."

Darith nodded. "That's the real danger. He doesn't just want soldiers - he wants devotion."

Kaelion's mind raced as he tried to piece together what they were facing. The Reaver wasn't like Cyrix; his power wasn't driven by ambition or madness alone. It was something deeper, more insidious - a force that could bend even the strongest wills to its cause.

"We need to act," he said, his voice low but firm. "If he finishes building that army, there won't be a realm left standing."

Selara's brow furrowed. "And how exactly do you plan to stop him? We don't have the shards anymore, Kaelion. We're fighting blind."

"Not entirely," Darith said. "There's something he doesn't know about. Something that might give us a chance."

Kaelion turned to him, his expression sharp. "What is it?"

Darith hesitated, his gaze flicking toward the camp. "There's a relic hidden deep in the Umbral Depths. It's older than the Axis - older than the shards. The legends say it can sever the bonds between light and shadow, breaking their influence entirely."

Selara's eyes narrowed. "And you think this relic can stop him?"

Darith shrugged. "I think it's our best shot."

Kaelion glanced at Selara, their eyes meeting in silent agreement. "Then we go after it."

The group retreated from the camp, moving swiftly through the rolling hills of the Marches. The Eclipse's light cast long shadows across the landscape, their movements concealed by the twilight haze.

As they traveled, Darith explained the relic's origins.

"It's called the Severance Stone," he said, his voice hushed as though speaking the name too loudly might summon its power. "The stories say it was forged in the first days of the realms, before the Axis existed. It's said to hold the power to unmake creation itself."

Kaelion frowned. "And you think it's just sitting there, waiting for us to find it?"

Darith's expression darkened. "If it's still there, it won't be unguarded. The Depths are full of things that were never meant to see the light."

Selara smirked faintly. "Sounds like home."

The Umbral Depths loomed ahead, their entrance a jagged maw in the side of a craggy hillside. Faint glimmers of bioluminescent light seeped from within, casting the shadows in eerie patterns.

Darith stopped at the threshold, his hand resting on the hilt of his blade. "This is where I leave you. The Depths aren't a place for outsiders."

Kaelion's brow furrowed. "You're not coming with us?"

Darith shook his head. "I've already risked too much just by telling you about the Stone. The Reaver's spies are everywhere. If they find out what you're after..."

Selara raised an eyebrow. "They'll what? Come after us harder?"

Darith met her gaze, his expression grave. "They'll do worse than kill you. The Reaver's power doesn't just take lives - it takes everything that makes you who you are."

Kaelion nodded slowly. "We'll manage."

Darith hesitated, then extended a hand. "Good luck. You'll need it."

Kaelion shook his hand, his grip firm. "Stay safe."

As Kaelion and Selara entered the Depths, the air grew colder, the shadows thicker. The faint hum of the Axis's energy that had once comforted Kaelion was gone, replaced by a deep, resonant silence.

Selara moved ahead, her steps light and deliberate. "Feels just like I remember," she said, her voice tinged with a mix of nostalgia and unease.

Kaelion followed, his hand resting on his sword. "Let's hope your memory is good enough to get us through this."

Selara smirked faintly. "Don't worry, knight. I've got this."

But as they delved deeper into the shadows, the air grew heavier, and the path ahead seemed to twist and shift, as though the Depths themselves were alive.

And somewhere, in the darkness, something stirred.

Chapter Three: The Living Shadows

The Umbral Depths welcomed them with a silence that was alive. The faint glimmers of bioluminescent fungi dotted the cavern walls, their cool blue light casting long, shifting shadows across the jagged stone. The path ahead was narrow and uneven, twisting and turning like a serpent burrowing deep into the earth.

Kaelion adjusted his grip on his sword, its weight reassuring in the oppressive darkness. "This place feels wrong," he muttered.

Selara, walking a few steps ahead, smirked without looking back. "You'd feel wrong too if you'd spent your existence buried under a city that tried to wipe you out."

Her voice was light, but Kaelion caught the edge of something deeper - resentment, or maybe grief. He didn't press. Selara's connection to the Depths was as much a part of her as his exile was of him, and neither was a topic to broach lightly.

The air grew colder as they descended, the faint hum of shadow magic becoming more pronounced. Kaelion's steps faltered when he felt the vibration through his boots, a rhythmic pulse that seemed to echo his heartbeat.

"You feel that?" he asked, his voice low.

Selara stopped, her head tilting slightly as if listening to something beyond the range of human hearing. "It's the Depths," she said after a moment. "They... remember."

Kaelion frowned. "Remember what?"

Selara turned to face him, her expression unreadable in the dim light. "Everything."

The path opened into a vast chamber, its ceiling lost in shadow. Stalactites dripped with glowing liquid, the faint plinks of water echoing across the cavern. The floor was uneven, dotted with pools of ink-like shadow that rippled as they walked past.

Kaelion's unease grew. He could feel the presence of something unseen, a weight pressing against his chest.

Selara knelt beside one of the pools, her hand hovering above its surface. The shadows swirled in response, forming shapes that dissolved as quickly as they appeared.

"They're restless," she murmured.

"Restless?" Kaelion asked, his hand tightening on his sword.

Selara straightened, her expression wary. "The Depths are alive, in a way. The shadows here remember everyone who's walked this path, every shard-bearer who's tried to claim its secrets. And they don't forget."

As if in response to her words, the air grew colder. The shadows on the walls began to shift, their movements too deliberate to be natural.

Kaelion's grip on his sword tightened. "Are we being watched?"

Selara didn't answer. Her eyes were fixed on the shifting shadows, her stance tense.

The first attack came without warning.

A shadow lunged from the wall, its form coalescing into a jagged, humanoid shape with claws like obsidian blades. Kaelion reacted instinctively, raising his sword to block as the creature struck with inhuman speed. The clash of steel against shadow rang through the cavern, and Kaelion felt the impact reverberate through his arms.

Selara moved with practiced precision, her hands weaving patterns in the air. The shadows around her responded, lashing out at the creature with sharp tendrils that wrapped around its limbs.

"Don't let it touch you!" she shouted.

Kaelion pushed back against the creature, his sword glowing faintly with the residual energy of the Axis. The light seemed to repel the shadow, but not for long. It recoiled, then surged forward again, its movements erratic but terrifyingly fast.

Selara's shadows tightened their grip, pulling the creature back. With a final swing, Kaelion's blade cut through it, and the creature dissolved into a swirling pool of darkness.

The silence that followed was short-lived.

All around them, the shadows began to move. One by one, figures emerged from the walls, their forms shifting and unstable.

"More of them," Kaelion muttered.

Selara's jaw tightened. "They're not just creatures. They're memories. Echoes of everyone who's ever tried to take the Severance Stone."

Kaelion's eyes darted around the chamber, counting at least a dozen shadow-forms closing in on them. "And what happens if we don't stop them?"

"They take everything," Selara said simply.

The battle was chaotic. The shadow-forms moved with relentless speed, their shapes shifting with each attack. Kaelion and Selara fought side by side, their movements in sync despite the overwhelming odds.

Kaelion's sword cleaved through one creature after another, the blade glowing brighter with each strike. But the shadows kept coming, their numbers seemingly endless.

Selara's shadows lashed out in sharp, precise strikes, holding the creatures at bay. Her control was masterful, but Kaelion could see the strain in her movements - the toll it was taking.

"We can't keep this up," he said between breaths.

"We don't have to," Selara replied, her voice tight. "We just need to get to the other side."

Kaelion glanced toward the far end of the chamber, where a narrow passageway led deeper into the Depths. The problem was the swarm of shadow-forms standing between them and their escape.

"Any ideas?" he asked.

Selara's lips curved into a faint smirk. "One. But you're not going to like it."

Selara stepped forward, raising her arms as if commanding the shadows around her. The air grew heavier, and the shadows hesitated, their movements slowing as if confused.

Kaelion realized what she was doing a second too late. "Selara - "

"Go!" she shouted.

The shadows converged on her, drawn to the energy she was wielding. Kaelion hesitated, his instincts screaming at him to stay, but he knew she was buying him time.

Gritting his teeth, he turned and ran toward the passageway, his heart pounding with every step. The shadows roared behind him, their cries echoing through the chamber as they swarmed around Selara.

Kaelion reached the passage and turned back, his breath catching as he saw Selara's form wreathed in shadows. She stood tall, her hands moving in intricate patterns as she held the creatures at bay.

"Selara!" he shouted.

She didn't look at him, her focus unbroken. "Find the Stone, Kaelion. Stop the Reaver."

Kaelion clenched his fists, his chest tightening as he turned and plunged deeper into the Depths.

Behind him, the shadows closed in.

Chapter Four: The Depths Remember

Kaelion moved through the narrow passage, the echoes of Selara's battle fading behind him. The oppressive silence of the Depths closed in, broken only by the sound of his footsteps and the faint hum of energy that seemed to resonate from the stone itself.

His grip tightened on his sword, the blade still faintly glowing from the earlier battle. He couldn't stop thinking about Selara, her silhouette engulfed by the shadows as she held them back. The memory gnawed at him, but he forced himself forward.

"Find the Stone. Stop the Reaver."

Her words rang in his ears, spurring him onward. The air grew colder, the weight of the Depths pressing down on him like a physical force. The light from the bioluminescent fungi dimmed, replaced by faint, swirling patterns etched into the walls - shapes that seemed to move if he looked too closely.

The passage opened into another chamber, this one smaller but more intricate. The walls were covered in carvings, each depicting scenes of conflict and unity. Figures of light and shadow clashed in endless cycles, their forms entwined in a dance of creation and destruction.

Kaelion approached one of the carvings, his eyes drawn to its details. A figure stood at the center, holding a crystalline object that radiated light and shadow. The Severance Stone.

So close, yet so far.

The hum of energy grew louder, and Kaelion's gaze snapped to the far side of the chamber. A massive, ornate door loomed before him, its surface inlaid with veins of glowing shadowlight. The patterns on the door pulsed faintly, as if alive, and a symbol at its center mirrored the design of the Severance Stone.

Kaelion's chest tightened. He reached for the door, his hand hovering over the symbol. The air around him seemed to shift, growing heavier with each passing moment.

As his fingers brushed the surface, a voice echoed through the chamber, low and resonant.

"Why do you seek the Stone?"

Kaelion froze. The voice seemed to come from everywhere and nowhere at once, vibrating through the stone and into his chest.

"I'm here to stop the Reaver," he said, his voice steady despite the weight of the words. "He's using the shards' corruption to build an army. If I don't stop him, the world won't survive."

The voice was silent for a moment, as if considering his response.

"And you believe the Stone will save you?"

Kaelion frowned. "If it can sever the bonds of light and shadow, it's the only chance we have."

The voice shifted, its tone sharpening. "The Stone does not choose lightly. Those who seek its power must first prove their worth."

The ground beneath Kaelion's feet trembled, and the door before him pulsed brighter. Shadows seeped from its edges, swirling into the air and taking form.

Kaelion stepped back, raising his sword as the shadows coalesced into a towering figure. Its shape was indistinct, shifting between humanoid and monstrous, but its presence was undeniable.

"Prove yourself," the voice commanded.

The shadow creature lunged, its massive claws swiping through the air with terrifying speed. Kaelion dodged to the side, his boots skidding on the uneven stone. He swung his sword, the blade cutting through the creature's form, but the shadows reformed almost instantly.

The creature struck again, its movements faster, more deliberate. Kaelion blocked the blow, the impact reverberating through his arms. The force drove him back, and he stumbled, barely managing to stay on his feet.

"You can't be defeated, can you?" Kaelion muttered through gritted teeth.

The creature lunged again, and Kaelion rolled to the side, the claws narrowly missing him. He pushed himself up, his mind racing. The carvings on the walls caught his eye, their patterns swirling with light and shadow.

The answer wasn't in brute force. It was in balance.

Kaelion steadied his breath, lowering his sword slightly as he studied the creature's movements. It struck again, and this time, he didn't dodge. Instead, he stepped into the attack, his blade meeting the creature's claws with precision. The impact sent a shockwave through the chamber, but Kaelion stood firm.

The creature hesitated, its form flickering. Kaelion moved quickly, weaving around its next attack and striking at its core - not with the intent to destroy, but to disrupt.

The creature staggered, its form unraveling slightly. Kaelion pressed forward, his strikes precise and controlled, each one aimed at maintaining the delicate balance between light and shadow.

Finally, the creature let out a low, resonant growl, its form dissolving into tendrils of darkness that faded into the walls.

The voice returned, softer now. "You understand. Balance is not achieved through force, but through harmony."

Kaelion exhaled heavily, his grip on his sword relaxing. "Does that mean I've proven myself?"

The door before him pulsed again, its veins of shadowlight glowing brighter. Slowly, it began to open, the stone groaning as it revealed a passage beyond.

"The Stone awaits. But be warned: its power is not yours to claim. It is yours to serve."

Kaelion stepped through the doorway, the air growing colder as he moved deeper into the Depths. The passage ahead was narrow, its walls lined with intricate patterns that glowed faintly in the darkness.

At the end of the passage, a soft light emanated from a pedestal, its glow illuminating the chamber beyond. Kaelion's breath caught as he approached, his eyes locking onto the object resting atop the pedestal.

The Severance Stone.

It was smaller than he'd imagined, a crystalline shard that pulsed with an inner light, its surface shifting between shades of gold and violet. The energy it emitted was overwhelming, a constant hum that resonated in his chest.

Kaelion hesitated, his hand hovering over the Stone.

"Find the Stone. Stop the Reaver."

Selara's words echoed in his mind, and he clenched his jaw, reaching out to take it.

The moment his fingers touched its surface, the chamber erupted in light and shadow, the two forces intertwining in a chaotic dance. Kaelion felt the power surge through him, a wave of energy that threatened to tear him apart.

The world around him dissolved into blinding light.

Chapter Five: The Burden of Power

Blinding light enveloped Kaelion, a chaotic swirl of gold and violet that seemed to stretch infinitely in every direction. He couldn't tell if his feet were on solid ground or if he was suspended in the ether. The Severance Stone pulsed in his hand, its energy coursing through him like molten fire.

The sensation was unbearable. His heart pounded as the currents of light and shadow intertwined, crashing against each other and threatening to rip him apart. He fell to his knees, gasping as his vision blurred and the weight of the Stone pressed down on his soul.

A voice echoed through the void - ancient and commanding, yet calm.

"You have touched the Severance Stone, bearer. But to wield its power is to understand its cost. Are you prepared to face the truth?"

Kaelion's fingers tightened around the Stone, his knuckles white. "I don't care about the cost," he said through gritted teeth. "I have to stop the Reaver."

The voice was silent for a moment, as though weighing his words.

"Very well. Then see what lies within."

The light around Kaelion shifted, coalescing into shapes and images that swirled past him like a storm. He saw visions of the past - the Axis splintering into shards, their fragments raining down across the realms. He saw Solaris Citadel basking in eternal light, its beauty masking the corruption beneath. He saw the Umbral Depths consumed by shadows, their once-great artistry turned to ash.

Then came the future.

Fires consumed the Twilight Marches as armies clashed beneath the Eclipse's pale glow. The Reaver stood at the heart of the chaos, his form towering and wreathed in a storm of light and shadow. Behind him, a massive rift tore through the sky, its edges crackling with raw energy.

Kaelion's heart sank as he watched the rift expand, its tendrils reaching out to engulf the realms. The balance they had fought so hard to restore was unraveling, replaced by a force of pure entropy.

The visions faded, leaving Kaelion trembling in the void.

"This is what awaits," the voice said. "The Severance Stone can stop the Reaver. But to do so, it will demand more than your strength - it will demand your very essence."

Kaelion forced himself to his feet, his grip on the Stone unyielding. "If that's what it takes, so be it."

The voice softened, almost mournful. "Very well. The Stone is yours, but its power will not be a gift. It will be a burden."

The light surged again, and the void collapsed around him.

Kaelion awoke on the cold stone floor of the chamber, the Severance Stone still clutched in his hand. Its glow had dimmed, but he could feel its presence - a steady hum of energy that pulsed in time with his heartbeat.

He pushed himself to his feet, his body aching from the ordeal. The air in the chamber was still, the oppressive weight of the Depths momentarily lifted.

Kaelion turned the Stone over in his hand, studying its crystalline surface. It no longer felt like a relic - it felt alive, its energy coursing through him like a second heartbeat.

As he stepped toward the passage leading out of the chamber, the ground beneath him rumbled. The walls trembled, and the patterns etched into the stone began to shift, their glowing lines converging into a single point.

A voice echoed from the depths of the passage - a voice that was unmistakable.

"Kaelion."

He froze. The voice was low, resonant, and laced with shadow.

Cyrix.

Kaelion's grip on the Stone tightened as he moved cautiously toward the sound. The passage twisted and turned, its walls narrowing as the air grew colder. The faint glow of the Severance Stone lit his path, its light casting jagged shadows that seemed to shift with each step.

At the end of the passage, the air opened into a wide chamber. And there, standing in the center, was Cyrix.

The former scholar-turned-zealot was a shadow of his former self. His armor was fractured and jagged, pulsating with the remnants of shard energy. His eyes glowed faintly, a mix of gold and violet that mirrored the Severance Stone.

Kaelion drew his sword, his stance steady. "Cyrix."

Cyrix turned to face him, a slow, deliberate movement. A faint smile curved his lips. "Kaelion. I was wondering when you'd arrive."

Kaelion's jaw tightened. "You're alive."

Cyrix spread his arms, his voice calm but filled with menace. "Alive... reborn... what does it matter? The shards may be gone, but their echoes remain. And through them, so do I."

Kaelion stepped forward, his sword at the ready. "You're the one behind the Reaver."

Cyrix chuckled, the sound low and unsettling. "Behind him? No, Kaelion. I am the Reaver."

The air around him rippled, and the energy emanating from his form surged. The shadows in the chamber coiled and twisted, responding to his presence.

"You reforged the Axis," Cyrix said, his tone mocking. "You thought the Eclipse was the end of the story. But it was only the beginning. Balance is weakness, Kaelion. Strength lies in dominion. And through the Severance Stone, I will achieve it."

Kaelion's grip on the Stone tightened, its energy surging through him as if in defiance of Cyrix's words.

"You won't win," Kaelion said, his voice steady. "The Axis was restored because we chose balance. You're nothing but a shadow trying to rewrite the truth."

Cyrix's smile widened, his form growing darker and more chaotic. "Then show me, Kaelion. Show me the strength of your so-called balance."

The shadows erupted, and the chamber descended into chaos.

Chapter Six: Clash of Wills

The shadows surged like a living tide, filling the chamber with chaos. Kaelion barely had time to react as a tendril of darkness lashed toward him, its edges sharp as razors. He rolled to the side, the Severance Stone glowing faintly in his hand, its energy rippling through his body in steady waves.

"Still quick, I see," Cyrix said, his voice echoing through the cavern. "But you'll find that speed alone won't save you."

Kaelion pushed to his feet, his sword raised. "I didn't come here to save myself."

Cyrix smirked, his form wreathed in shadows that shifted and coiled with unnatural precision. "No, you came to stop me. But tell me, Kaelion, do you even know what that means? Do you understand the power you hold?"

Kaelion didn't answer. Instead, he lunged, his sword cutting through the shadows with a burst of light. The blow connected with Cyrix's armor, but the impact barely seemed to faze him. The shadows around him absorbed the energy, twisting and reforming as Cyrix stepped back, his expression calm.

"Predictable," Cyrix said. "You wield the Severance Stone like a child with a toy. Its power isn't meant for destruction. It's meant for domination."

Cyrix raised his hand, and the chamber trembled. Shadows erupted from the walls, their forms coalescing into jagged constructs that moved with terrifying speed. Kaelion dodged as one lunged at him, its claws raking the ground where he'd stood a moment before.

The Severance Stone pulsed in his hand, its energy surging as Kaelion focused. He swung his sword, the blade glowing with the Stone's light. The construct shattered on impact, its pieces dissolving into mist.

Cyrix watched with mild interest. "You've improved. But you still lack understanding."

Kaelion gritted his teeth, his chest heaving as he turned to face Cyrix. "The only thing I need to understand is how to stop you."

Cyrix laughed, the sound low and resonant. "Stop me? You can't stop what I've become. The shards gave me their power, and the Severance Stone will complete my transformation. Through it, I'll do what the Axis couldn't - remake this world in my image."

Kaelion's grip on the Stone tightened. "And you think that's strength? Forcing the world to bend to your will?"

Cyrix's eyes gleamed, their light a mix of gold and violet. "Strength is all that matters. The Eclipse was a mistake, Kaelion. Balance is weakness masquerading as order. True power lies in control."

The chamber grew darker as Cyrix extended his hand, the shadows responding to his command. A massive wave of darkness surged toward Kaelion, its edges bristling with shards of jagged energy.

Kaelion held his ground, the Severance Stone glowing brighter in his hand. He focused its energy, channeling it into his sword. The blade flared with light, and he swung it in a wide arc, the strike splitting the wave in two.

The force of the impact sent Kaelion stumbling back, but he recovered quickly, his eyes fixed on Cyrix.

"You talk about power like it's something you can own," Kaelion said, his voice steady. "But real strength isn't about control. It's about choice. It's about knowing when to stand and when to step aside."

Cyrix's expression darkened. "Spare me your philosophy, knight. You had your chance to shape this world, and you failed. Now, it's my turn."

The battle raged on, each clash of light and shadow shaking the chamber. Kaelion moved with precision, his strikes guided by the Severance Stone's energy. But Cyrix's power was overwhelming, his mastery of the shadows unmatched.

Kaelion's chest burned with exertion, and the weight of the Stone's power grew heavier with each passing moment. He could feel it pulling at him, testing his resolve, tempting him with the promise of greater strength.

"You feel it, don't you?" Cyrix said, his voice cutting through the chaos. "The Stone is calling to you. It knows your fears, your doubts. Embrace them, and you'll see the truth."

Kaelion's grip on the Stone faltered for a moment, the temptation seeping into his mind. Images flashed before him - visions of his failures, his regrets. The innocent lives he couldn't save. The allies he'd lost.

He shook his head, forcing the images away. "I won't let it control me."

Cyrix's laugh echoed through the chamber. "Control? No, Kaelion. It's not about control. It's about acceptance. Accept your fears, and you'll find your true strength."

Kaelion steadied himself, his breath coming in ragged gasps. The Severance Stone pulsed in his hand, its energy fluctuating as though responding to his resolve.

He closed his eyes, focusing on the rhythm of the Stone's power. It wasn't just light or shadow - it was both, intertwined in a delicate balance. The answer wasn't in resisting its influence or giving in to its temptation. It was in understanding it.

When Kaelion opened his eyes, they glowed faintly with the Stone's light. He stepped forward, his movements deliberate. Cyrix's smirk faltered as Kaelion raised his sword, the blade radiating with the combined energy of light and shadow.

"You think strength is about domination," Kaelion said, his voice steady. "But you're wrong. True strength is knowing when to let go."

With a surge of energy, Kaelion brought his sword down, the strike unleashing a wave of balanced energy that tore through the chamber.

Cyrix roared as the energy collided with him, the shadows around him unraveling. The chamber shook violently, and cracks spread across the walls as the light of the Severance Stone consumed the darkness.

When the dust settled, Cyrix was gone.

Kaelion stood alone in the chamber, the Severance Stone dimming in his hand. The air was still, the oppressive weight of the Depths lifted. He lowered his sword, his chest heaving as he took in the silence.

But the victory felt hollow. Cyrix's final words echoed in his mind, a lingering reminder that the battle was far from over.

"You had your chance to shape this world, and you failed. Now, it's my turn."

Kaelion tightened his grip on the Stone, his resolve hardening. The Reaver's threat wasn't over, and the cost of stopping him would demand more than he'd ever imagined.

He turned toward the passage leading out of the chamber, the faint glow of the Eclipse guiding his path.

The fight was only beginning.

Chapter Seven: Echoes of the Reaver

Kaelion emerged from the chamber into a corridor shrouded in silence. The Severance Stone's faint glow lit his path, its energy pulsating rhythmically, still intertwined with the power he had wielded against Cyrix. His legs felt heavy, each step dragging under the weight of exhaustion and uncertainty.

The Depths felt different now, quieter, but not in a way that comforted him. The living shadows that had previously moved with a restless purpose were still, their shapes lingering in the periphery of his vision like watchers.

Selara's face flashed in his mind, her last words hanging over him like an unfinished sentence.

"Find the Stone. Stop the Reaver."

He gritted his teeth, forcing himself forward.

The passage opened into a familiar cavern, the bioluminescent fungi casting their cool glow against the jagged stone. The sight of it sent a wave of relief through Kaelion - he had made it back to where they had first split. But the relief was short-lived.

The shadows moved.

Kaelion froze, his hand tightening on his sword. From the far side of the cavern, a figure emerged, its steps deliberate and slow.

"Kaelion."

Selara.

Her form was wreathed in shadows, but it was her. Her violet eyes glinted in the faint light, their sharpness tempered by something... darker.

Kaelion lowered his sword slightly, his heart sinking. "Selara? You're alive?"

She tilted her head, her voice calm but cold. "Alive? I suppose you could call it that."

Something was wrong. Her movements were too smooth, her voice too detached. The shadows around her swirled unnaturally, coiling like snakes at her feet.

"What happened to you?" Kaelion asked, stepping closer.

Selara's lips curled into a faint smile, but it didn't reach her eyes. "The Depths remember, Kaelion. And they remembered me."

Kaelion stopped a few paces away, his sword still lowered but ready. "Selara, we need to leave. The Reaver - Cyrix - isn't finished. There's more coming."

Selara's smile widened. "Oh, Kaelion. You still think this is about Cyrix? About stopping him?"

Her tone sent a chill down his spine.

"The Severance Stone," she continued, her gaze dropping to the glowing shard in his hand. "You think it's the answer. But it's not. It's just another piece of a puzzle we were never meant to solve."

Kaelion shook his head. "Selara, this isn't you. The shadows - "

"The shadows are part of me," she interrupted, her voice rising. "They've always been part of me. I just didn't see it until now."

She stepped closer, and Kaelion's grip on his sword tightened. The shadows around her flared, reaching out like tendrils.

"The Reaver's vision isn't wrong, Kaelion," she said. "The world isn't meant to stay in balance. Light and shadow weren't made to coexist - they were made to fight. To test each other. That's where strength comes from."

Kaelion's chest tightened. "That's not true. Balance isn't weakness, Selara. It's what keeps us from tearing ourselves apart."

Her expression hardened, the shadows around her growing darker. "You've been blinded by the Eclipse. You think the Axis is whole, but it's still broken, Kaelion. And until we shatter it completely, this world will never be free."

Kaelion raised his sword, his heart heavy. "I won't let you do this."

Selara's eyes flashed. "Then you'll have to stop me."

The fight was swift and brutal.

Selara moved with the precision of a dancer, her shadows striking with deadly accuracy. Kaelion met each attack with equal skill, his sword glowing brighter as the Severance Stone's energy surged through him.

"Don't make me do this!" he shouted, his voice echoing through the cavern.

Selara's reply came as a whip of shadow that narrowly missed his face. "You already have, Kaelion."

Their movements were a blur, light and shadow clashing in bursts of energy that lit up the cavern. Each strike carried a weight far beyond the physical, their conflict steeped in years of shared pain and understanding.

Kaelion's blade finally found an opening, cutting through the shadows that encased Selara. She staggered back, her breath coming in sharp gasps.

But instead of retreating, she smiled - a broken, weary expression that cut deeper than any blade.

"You'll see," she whispered. "When the light fades, you'll see the truth."

The shadows around her surged, swallowing her form in an instant. Kaelion lunged, his hand outstretched, but it was too late. The darkness receded, and she was gone.

Kaelion stood alone in the cavern, his chest heaving as the Severance Stone's light dimmed. The silence was suffocating, broken only by the faint hum of the Depths.

He lowered his sword, his mind racing. Selara wasn't lost - not completely. But something had changed in her, something he didn't yet understand.

He turned toward the passage leading out of the Depths, his resolve hardening. The Severance Stone pulsed faintly in his hand, a reminder of the burden he carried.

The fight wasn't over.

It was only just beginning.

Chapter Eight: The Gathering Storm

The Twilight Marches stretched out before Kaelion as he emerged from the oppressive confines of the Umbral Depths. The faint light of the Eclipse illuminated the rolling hills and scattered camps, casting everything in muted hues of violet and gold. The air was crisp and cold, a stark contrast to the stifling atmosphere of the Depths.

Kaelion's steps faltered as he surveyed the distant camps. Smoke curled into the twilight sky from scattered fires, and faint voices carried on the wind - shouts, chants, and the unmistakable ring of steel. The clans were preparing for war.

He tightened his grip on the Severance Stone, its energy pulsing faintly against his palm. The memory of Selara's twisted smile haunted him, her words replaying in his mind like an echo.

"When the light fades, you'll see the truth."

Kaelion pushed the thought aside, focusing on the task ahead. If the Reaver was mobilizing the clans, there was little time to waste.

The camp ahead was larger than any Kaelion had seen since leaving Solaris Citadel. Rows of tents stretched across the hills, their banners bearing symbols of shadowlight. Warriors moved with purpose, their armor mismatched but their weapons sharp. The shard-forged blades glinted with a faint, ominous glow, a testament to the corruption that still lingered in the world.

Kaelion approached cautiously, keeping to the shadows of the hillside. He could hear the distant murmur of voices - a meeting, perhaps, or a rallying speech. He crept closer, his footsteps silent on the soft grass.

At the center of the camp, a large tent loomed, its entrance guarded by two heavily armed warriors. Kaelion's gaze flicked to the surrounding area, noting the patrols and clusters of soldiers. He would need a distraction to get inside.

The Severance Stone pulsed faintly in his hand, and Kaelion felt its energy ripple through him. It wasn't just power - it was a connection, a thread that tied him to the balance of light and shadow. He closed his eyes, focusing on the rhythm of the Stone's pulse.

A faint vibration spread through the ground, subtle but deliberate. The nearest firepit flared suddenly, the flames roaring to life and sending a plume of sparks into the air. Shouts of alarm erupted as warriors scrambled to contain the blaze.

Kaelion slipped past the guards, their attention diverted, and ducked into the tent.

The air inside was heavy with tension. A large table dominated the center of the space, its surface covered in maps and documents. Figures stood around it, their voices low and urgent.

At the head of the table stood a man Kaelion didn't recognize. His armor was dark and ornate, and his presence commanded the room. His voice was calm but sharp, cutting through the murmur of conversation.

"The Reaver's orders are clear," the man said. "We march at dawn. The Twilight Marches will fall, and the rest will follow."

Kaelion's heart sank. The Reaver's forces were already mobilizing, their plans set in motion.

He edged closer, his movements silent. He needed more information - something that could give him an advantage.

The conversation continued, the warriors discussing supply routes and battle strategies. Kaelion listened intently, memorizing their plans.

But then, the man at the head of the table paused, his gaze shifting.

"Someone's here," he said, his voice cold.

Kaelion froze.

The man's eyes scanned the tent, his expression hardening. He gestured to the others, and the warriors drew their weapons, fanning out to search the space.

Kaelion cursed under his breath, gripping his sword tightly. He moved quickly, slipping behind a stack of crates as the warriors closed in.

The Severance Stone pulsed again, its energy humming in his chest. Kaelion focused, channeling the Stone's power. A faint ripple spread through the air, distorting the shadows in the tent.

The warriors hesitated, their movements faltering as the shadows shifted unnaturally. One of them raised his weapon, his eyes darting nervously.

"What's happening?" he muttered.

Kaelion used the distraction to his advantage. He moved swiftly, striking with precision. His blade caught one warrior in the side, the strike silent but effective. The man crumpled, and Kaelion moved to the next, his movements fluid and controlled.

The tent erupted into chaos as the remaining warriors turned on him, their weapons flashing in the dim light. Kaelion parried their attacks, his sword glowing faintly as the Severance Stone's energy flowed through it.

The leader barked orders, his voice sharp. "Take him alive!"

Kaelion gritted his teeth, his strikes becoming more deliberate. He couldn't afford to be captured - not now, not when so much was at stake.

The battle was short but brutal. Kaelion stood over the fallen warriors, his breath coming in ragged gasps. The leader remained, his sword raised, his eyes cold and calculating.

"You're brave," the man said, his voice calm despite the tension in the air. "But bravery won't save you."

Kaelion leveled his sword, his stance steady. "I don't need saving."

The man's smirk was brief but dangerous. He lunged, his blade striking with the precision of a seasoned fighter. Kaelion met the attack head-on, their swords clashing in a burst of sparks.

The Severance Stone pulsed again, its energy surging through Kaelion's blade. He pushed back against the man's strength, forcing him to retreat.

"You don't know what you're fighting for," the man said, his tone edged with disdain. "The Reaver's vision is the only future this world has. The Eclipse was a lie - a fleeting illusion of peace. Strength is the only truth."

Kaelion's jaw tightened. "Strength doesn't come from domination. It comes from standing together."

The man's eyes narrowed, but before he could respond, Kaelion moved. His strike was swift and final, his blade cutting through the man's defenses. The leader fell, his weapon clattering to the ground.

Kaelion exhaled heavily, the tension in his chest easing slightly.

The tent was quiet now, the maps and documents scattered in the aftermath of the fight. Kaelion knelt, sifting through the papers for anything useful.

His gaze settled on a map marked with symbols he didn't recognize. A faint glow emanated from one of the markings, its energy similar to the Severance Stone's pulse.

Kaelion frowned, his fingers brushing the map. Whatever the Reaver was planning, it centered on this location.

He folded the map and tucked it into his cloak. As he turned to leave, the Severance Stone pulsed again, its energy steady and insistent.

Kaelion stepped out into the night, the faint hum of the Eclipse guiding his path.

The storm was coming.

Chapter Nine: The Mark of the Stone

The chill of the Eclipse night followed Kaelion as he descended the hill, the enemy camp receding into the distance. The map he'd taken was tucked securely in his cloak, its cryptic markings burned into his memory. His mind raced with the implications of what he'd seen: the Reaver's forces were mobilizing, and whatever power they sought at the map's glowing location would tip the scales irrevocably.

The Severance Stone pulsed faintly in his hand, its rhythm steady but insistent. It seemed to hum with a life of its own, urging him forward yet warning him of the path ahead.

Kaelion's muscles ached, but he pressed on, the weight of the Stone in his grip both a burden and a promise. He had no time to rest - not when the Reaver's vision of domination loomed closer with each passing moment.

By dawn, Kaelion reached a secluded glade at the edge of the Twilight Marches. The soft glow of the stardust grass gave the area an otherworldly beauty, but Kaelion's senses remained sharp. He wasn't alone.

A figure emerged from the shadows, their movements deliberate but unthreatening. Kaelion tensed, his hand moving instinctively to the hilt of his sword.

"Easy," the figure said, their voice calm and familiar.

Darith stepped into the light, his weathered face marked with exhaustion. His cloak bore the emblem of the Silverveil clan, but his eyes were sharper than Kaelion remembered.

"You've been busy," Darith said, his gaze dropping to the Severance Stone in Kaelion's hand.

Kaelion nodded, his grip on the Stone tightening. "The Reaver's forces are moving. They're after something - something tied to this." He pulled the map from his cloak, unfolding it and showing the glowing marking. "What do you know about this place?"

Darith's expression darkened as he studied the map. "The Hollow Spire," he said after a moment. "It's an ancient site, older than the Axis. The legends say it's where light and shadow first converged, where the balance was forged."

Kaelion frowned. "And the Reaver wants to break that balance."

Darith nodded grimly. "If he succeeds, the world won't survive what comes next."

The wind shifted, carrying the faint sound of approaching footsteps. Kaelion and Darith exchanged a glance, their instincts aligning.

"Move," Darith said, his voice low.

Kaelion followed him into the trees, the map tucked securely in his cloak. They moved swiftly but quietly, weaving through the dense foliage as the sound of the enemy patrol grew louder.

The Severance Stone pulsed in Kaelion's hand, its energy resonating with the approaching presence. Kaelion paused, his eyes narrowing as he scanned the area.

"They're close," he muttered.

Darith drew his blade, its edge dull but deadly. "Then let's hope they're not expecting us."

The patrol emerged into view - a group of five soldiers, their shard-forged weapons glinting in the faint light. They moved with purpose, their formation tight and disciplined.

Kaelion signaled to Darith, the two of them circling around the soldiers with practiced precision. The Severance Stone's energy hummed in Kaelion's chest, steadying his movements.

The first soldier fell before he realized he was under attack, Kaelion's blade striking with silent efficiency. The others reacted quickly, their weapons raised as they turned toward the sound.

Darith charged from the other side, his blade cutting through a second soldier with ruthless precision. The remaining three closed ranks, their weapons glowing with shard energy as they advanced.

Kaelion met them head-on, his sword clashing against the nearest soldier's blade. The impact sent a jolt up his arm, but he held his ground, countering with a quick strike that left his opponent staggered.

Darith moved with deadly efficiency, his strikes precise and brutal. The soldiers fought with determination, but their numbers quickly dwindled under the combined assault.

The last soldier fell with a sharp cry, his weapon clattering to the ground. Kaelion exhaled heavily, the tension in his chest easing slightly as he surveyed the aftermath.

Darith wiped his blade on the grass, his expression grim. "The Reaver's influence is spreading faster than I thought."

Kaelion nodded, his grip on the Severance Stone tightening. "We need to move. If they know about the Hollow Spire, they'll send more."

The journey to the Hollow Spire was treacherous. The terrain grew harsher as they traveled deeper into the Twilight Marches, the ground turning rocky and uneven. The Eclipse's light cast long, jagged shadows across the landscape, and the air grew colder with each passing hour.

The Severance Stone pulsed faintly, its rhythm steady but ominous. Kaelion could feel its energy growing stronger as they neared their destination, the connection between the Stone and the Spire undeniable.

By the time the Spire came into view, the sunless sky had turned a deeper shade of violet. The towering structure loomed in the distance, its silhouette jagged and unnatural. Veins of glowing light and shadow ran through its surface, their patterns shifting like living things.

Darith stopped, his gaze fixed on the Spire. "We're too late," he said, his voice heavy.

Kaelion followed his gaze, his stomach sinking. The base of the Spire was swarming with activity - warriors clad in shard-forged armor, their weapons gleaming with unnatural energy.

At the center of the gathering stood a figure Kaelion recognized instantly.

Selara.

She moved with purpose, her violet eyes glowing faintly as she directed the warriors. The shadows around her coiled and shifted, responding to her presence like extensions of her will.

Kaelion's chest tightened, his grip on the Severance Stone faltering.

"She's leading them," Darith said, his voice low.

Kaelion nodded, his jaw clenched. "And she's not the only one."

Beyond Selara, standing at the base of the Spire, was a second figure - taller, clad in jagged armor that radiated a mix of light and shadow.

Cyrix.

Kaelion's breath caught as he watched the two figures confer, their postures commanding and resolute. Whatever plan they were enacting, it was already in motion.

Darith turned to Kaelion, his expression grave. "What now?"

Kaelion's gaze remained fixed on Selara and Cyrix. The Severance Stone pulsed in his hand, its energy flaring as though in defiance of the scene before him.

"Now," Kaelion said, his voice steady, "we end this."

Chapter Ten: The Hollow Spire

The Hollow Spire loomed like a jagged scar against the violet sky, its surface alive with veins of shifting light and shadow. The energy emanating from the structure was palpable, vibrating through the ground and the air alike. Kaelion stood at the edge of the ridge, his gaze fixed on the gathering below.

Warriors swarmed the base of the Spire, their shard-forged weapons glinting ominously. At their center stood Selara and Cyrix, their forms stark against the Spire's chaotic glow. They commanded the battlefield like twin harbingers, their presence sending ripples of tension through the gathered forces.

Darith crouched beside Kaelion, his face pale and drawn. "They've fortified the area. If we try to go in directly, we'll be cut down before we reach the Spire."

Kaelion's hand tightened around the Severance Stone. Its energy pulsed in his grasp, surging faintly in response to the scene below. He could feel the Spire's resonance pulling at him, a connection that thrummed through every fiber of his being.

"We can't wait," Kaelion said, his voice steady despite the storm of doubt brewing in his mind. "If they activate whatever's inside that Spire, it's over."

Darith frowned. "And what's your plan? March down there and challenge both of them at once?"

Kaelion turned to him, his gaze hard. "If that's what it takes."

They approached the encampment under cover of the Eclipse's twilight haze. The terrain was uneven, dotted with jagged rocks that provided just enough cover to conceal their movements. Kaelion's senses were sharp, every sound and flicker of movement drawing his attention.

The Severance Stone pulsed with increasing intensity, its energy guiding him like a beacon. He could feel the Spire's power growing stronger as they drew closer, its presence a constant weight in the air.

"Kaelion," Darith whispered, his tone urgent.

Kaelion turned, following Darith's gaze to a group of patrolling warriors moving toward them. Their shard-forged armor shimmered faintly in the dim light, and their weapons crackled with raw energy.

"We'll have to take them out quietly," Darith said, his hand resting on the hilt of his blade.

Kaelion nodded. He adjusted his grip on his sword, the Severance Stone's light dimming as he focused its energy inward.

The fight was quick and silent.

Kaelion moved with precision, his blade striking true as he dispatched the first warrior. Darith followed suit, his movements efficient and calculated. The patrol never had a chance to raise an alarm, their bodies falling silently to the ground.

Kaelion wiped his blade clean, his gaze fixed on the path ahead. The Spire loomed closer now, its chaotic energy casting long, jagged shadows across the encampment.

"We're getting close," Darith said, his voice low. "But if they see us coming - "

"They won't," Kaelion interrupted. His jaw tightened as he turned to Darith. "I'll handle Selara. You focus on the Spire. If there's a way to stop whatever they're planning, find it."

Darith hesitated, his expression conflicted. "Are you sure? You might not - "

"I don't have a choice," Kaelion said, cutting him off. "Go."

Darith nodded reluctantly, his eyes lingering on Kaelion for a moment before he turned and disappeared into the shadows.

Kaelion took a deep breath, the Severance Stone pulsing in his hand. He stepped forward, his gaze fixed on the two figures standing at the base of the Spire.

Selara was the first to notice him. She turned, her violet eyes narrowing as Kaelion approached. The shadows around her coiled like living things, their movements mirroring her rising tension.

"Kaelion," she said, her voice cold and sharp. "I knew you'd come."

Cyrix turned slowly, his jagged armor glinting in the Spire's chaotic glow. His expression was calm, but his eyes burned with a dangerous intensity.

"Ah, the knight of balance," Cyrix said, his tone mocking. "Come to preach your philosophy again?"

Kaelion stopped a few paces away, his sword in one hand and the Severance Stone in the other. "I came to stop you. Both of you."

Selara's lips curled into a faint, bitter smile. "Stop us? You still don't understand, do you? This world isn't meant for balance. It's meant to be broken."

Kaelion's chest tightened. "You're wrong, Selara. The balance isn't a weakness - it's the only thing keeping this world from falling apart."

Cyrix laughed, the sound low and resonant. "The Eclipse was a fleeting dream, Kaelion. A fragile illusion. True strength lies in dominance. In control. And through the Spire, I will bring this world to its knees."

Kaelion raised his sword, his gaze unwavering. "Not while I'm still standing."

The battle began with a burst of energy.

Selara struck first, her shadows lashing out like whips. Kaelion parried the attack, his sword glowing with the Severance Stone's energy. The clash of light and shadow lit up the area, their movements a blur of precision and power.

Cyrix joined the fray, his strikes heavy and deliberate. Kaelion moved quickly, dodging and countering as the two enemies pressed their assault. The Severance Stone pulsed in his hand, its energy surging through him with each strike.

The fight was chaotic, each clash sending shockwaves through the air. Kaelion's focus wavered as he struggled to keep up with their relentless attacks.

"Give in, Kaelion," Selara said, her voice rising above the din. "The Stone doesn't belong to you. It never did."

Kaelion gritted his teeth, his chest heaving as he blocked another strike. "I won't let you destroy everything we've fought for."

Cyrix smirked, his movements steady and calculated. "And what have you fought for, Kaelion? A fleeting balance? A lie?"

Kaelion's sword flared with light as he lunged, his strike aimed at Cyrix's chest. The blow connected, sending Cyrix staggering back, but Selara was already moving. Her shadows coiled around Kaelion's legs, pulling him off balance.

He fell hard, the breath knocked from his lungs. The Severance Stone slipped from his grasp, its light flickering as it rolled across the ground.

Selara stepped closer, her violet eyes glowing faintly. She knelt, picking up the Stone and holding it in her hand.

"You've held this long enough," she said, her tone cold.

Kaelion struggled to rise, his vision blurring as Selara stood over him. Cyrix approached, his form wreathed in shadow, his smile sharp and predatory.

"It's over," Cyrix said, his voice triumphant.

Kaelion's fingers tightened around his sword, his resolve hardening. "Not yet."

Chapter Eleven: Fractured Light

The Severance Stone's glow pulsed faintly in Selara's hand, its rhythm mirroring the tension crackling in the air. Kaelion knelt on the ground, his breaths ragged, his sword trembling in his grasp. The weight of defeat pressed down on him, but deep within, a spark of resolve refused to extinguish.

Selara stood over him, her eyes glowing faintly with shadowlight. She turned the Stone over in her hand, studying its crystalline surface with a mix of reverence and bitterness.

"You held this like it was a burden," she said, her voice cold. "But it's not a curse, Kaelion. It's freedom. Power."

Cyrix stepped closer, his jagged armor radiating with a chaotic mix of light and shadow. "She's right, you know," he said, his tone dripping with mockery. "The Stone was never yours to wield. You've always been a pretender - a hollow knight clinging to a broken ideal."

Kaelion's jaw tightened, his grip on his sword steadying. "You think domination is strength? That tearing the world apart will make you whole?"

Cyrix's smile widened. "It's not about destruction. It's about perfection. The balance you cling to is nothing but a chain. The Spire will break it - and I will rebuild the world in my image."

Kaelion's gaze shifted to Selara. Her expression was unreadable, but the shadows around her coiled and writhed as though alive.

"Selara," Kaelion said, his voice softer. "This isn't you. You've always created, not destroyed. Don't let him use you to finish what he started."

For a moment, something flickered in her eyes - hesitation, doubt - but it vanished as quickly as it appeared.

"You don't understand," she said, her voice sharp. "The world doesn't need balance. It needs change. And this" - she held up the Severance Stone - "is how we make it happen."

The ground beneath them trembled, and the Hollow Spire pulsed with energy. The patterns running through its surface shifted, their glow intensifying as the connection between the Spire and the Stone grew stronger.

Cyrix's gaze turned toward the Spire, a satisfied smile spreading across his face. "It's almost time. Once the Spire's power is unleashed, there will be no going back."

Kaelion pushed himself to his feet, the weight of his exhaustion replaced by a fierce determination. His sword gleamed faintly, its light a defiant contrast to the growing shadows.

"I won't let you destroy everything," he said, his voice steady.

Cyrix turned back to him, his expression amused. "And what will you do, knight? Fight us both? You can't stop the inevitable."

Kaelion took a step forward, his gaze locking on Selara. "You've already won once, Cyrix. But this time, you won't take her with you."

Selara's eyes narrowed, but Kaelion caught the flicker of emotion in her expression.

Cyrix raised his hand, the shadows around him surging forward like a tidal wave. Kaelion braced himself, his sword glowing brighter as he channeled every ounce of the Severance Stone's lingering energy into his blade.

The shadows struck with relentless force, crashing against Kaelion's defenses. His movements were precise but desperate, each strike fueled by a mix of skill and sheer willpower.

"Selara!" he shouted, his voice cutting through the chaos. "You don't have to do this! You're stronger than he is - you always have been!"

Selara hesitated, her hand tightening around the Stone. The shadows around her faltered, their movements less deliberate.

Cyrix noticed the shift and turned to her, his tone sharp. "Don't listen to him. He doesn't see what you see. He'll only hold you back."

Kaelion lunged forward, his blade slicing through the shadows as he closed the distance between them. Selara's gaze snapped back to him, her expression torn.

"Selara," Kaelion said, his voice softer now. "You've always been more than your pain. Don't let him take that from you."

The Severance Stone flared brightly in Selara's hand, its energy surging as if responding to her turmoil. She took a step back, her breaths coming in sharp gasps as the light and shadow within the Stone warred for dominance.

Cyrix's expression darkened. "Enough!" he bellowed, his form swelling with power. He lunged at Kaelion, his blade slicing through the air with terrifying speed.

Kaelion met the attack head-on, their swords clashing in a burst of energy that sent shockwaves through the Spire. The ground trembled beneath them, cracks spreading across the stone as the Spire's glow intensified.

Selara stumbled back, the Severance Stone's energy growing uncontrollable in her grasp. She looked between Kaelion and Cyrix, her expression torn with conflict.

"You don't have to choose him," Kaelion said, his voice strained as he blocked another strike. "You can still choose yourself."

Selara's grip on the Stone faltered, and for a moment, the shadows around her stilled.

Cyrix snarled, his focus shifting to her. "Don't let him twist you. The power is yours - take it, and we'll finish this together!"

Selara's gaze dropped to the Stone, its glow pulsing with a mix of light and shadow. Her hand trembled as she stepped toward the center of the Spire, her movements deliberate but uncertain.

The Spire responded to her approach, its glow intensifying as tendrils of energy reached out toward the Stone. The air grew heavy, charged with a raw, untamed power that made Kaelion's chest tighten.

"Selara, no!" Kaelion shouted, his voice filled with desperation.

She stopped at the edge of the Spire's central platform, the Stone's light spilling across her face. She turned to Kaelion, her expression unreadable.

"I've made my choice," she said, her voice barely above a whisper.

She raised the Stone, and the Spire erupted with energy.

Chapter Twelve: Shattered Bonds

The Hollow Spire erupted in a maelstrom of energy. Veins of light and shadow surged across its jagged surface, intertwining in a chaotic dance. The Severance Stone pulsed in Selara's hand, its glow bright enough to eclipse the dim light of the realm itself.

Kaelion staggered as the ground trembled beneath him, the Spire's resonance overwhelming his senses. The air crackled with power, sharp and electric, filling his lungs with each breath.

"Selara, stop!" Kaelion shouted, his voice straining against the roar of the Spire's awakening.

Selara stood at the center of the platform, her silhouette stark against the storm of energy swirling around her. The Severance Stone hovered just above her outstretched hand, its light flickering with wild, unstable brilliance.

"This is the only way," Selara said, her voice calm yet resolute.

Cyrix stepped forward, his jagged armor shimmering with the same chaotic energy as the Spire. His eyes glowed with triumph, his voice cutting through the chaos. "Yes, Selara. Complete the connection. The world will bend, and we will shape it anew."

Kaelion raised his sword, its blade trembling in his grip. "Don't listen to him! The Spire isn't the answer - it's a trap. It'll destroy you!"

Selara's gaze shifted to Kaelion, her expression unreadable. For a moment, something flickered in her eyes - doubt, hesitation - but it was gone as quickly as it had appeared.

"You don't understand, Kaelion," she said. "The balance was never meant to last. Light and shadow aren't opposites - they're adversaries. The world has to break before it can heal."

The Spire's energy surged, and the tendrils of light and shadow extended further, reaching toward Selara like living things. Kaelion's heart raced as he took a step forward, his sword glowing faintly in the storm's chaotic light.

"If you do this," he said, his voice firm, "there won't be anything left to heal. The Spire will tear the Axis apart - and everything with it."

Cyrix laughed, a low, resonant sound that echoed through the trembling chamber. "And why should we fear that? Let the Axis fall. Let the shards scatter. We'll forge something greater from the ruins."

Kaelion gritted his teeth, his gaze fixed on Selara. "You're not him, Selara. You've always been more than destruction. Don't let him use you to finish what he started."

Selara hesitated, the Severance Stone trembling in her grasp. The shadows around her faltered, their movements slowing as though mirroring her conflict.

"Selara," Kaelion said, his voice softer now. "You have a choice."

Cyrix's expression darkened, his jagged form swelling with shadowlight. "Enough of this." He raised his hand, and a surge of energy shot toward Kaelion, sharp and blinding.

Kaelion barely had time to react. He raised his sword, the Severance Stone's lingering energy flaring as it absorbed the impact. The force drove him back, his boots skidding across the trembling ground.

Cyrix turned to Selara, his voice sharp and commanding. "End this, Selara. Break the balance. Take your place at my side, and we'll rebuild the world as it should be."

Selara's grip on the Stone tightened, her breathing shallow. The Spire's energy surged around her, its glow reflecting the storm within her.

"I... I don't know," she whispered, her voice trembling.

Kaelion steadied himself, his chest heaving. "You do know, Selara. You've always known. The world doesn't need domination - it needs you. The real you."

The Severance Stone's light flickered, its chaotic glow stabilizing for a moment. Selara looked down at it, her expression softening. The shadows around her stilled, their chaotic movements replaced by a quiet hum.

Cyrix stepped closer, his tone laced with venom. "Don't let him deceive you. Balance is a lie, Selara. Take the power. Finish what we started."

Kaelion took a step forward, his sword lowering slightly. "You're stronger than this, Selara. You don't need him. You don't need the Stone. You just need to be you."

Selara's breathing steadied, and she looked up, her gaze locking with Kaelion's. The flicker of doubt in her eyes was gone, replaced by something resolute.

"I'm sorry," she said softly.

Before either Kaelion or Cyrix could react, Selara raised the Severance Stone high above her head. The Spire's energy surged, its light and shadow converging in a brilliant, blinding explosion.

The force of the blast sent Kaelion flying, his body slamming into the ground as the world around him dissolved into chaos. Light and shadow clashed violently, their combined energy tearing through the air with a deafening roar.

Kaelion forced himself to his knees, his vision blurred by the intensity of the Spire's eruption. At the center of the platform, Selara stood wreathed in light and shadow, her form barely visible amidst the storm.

Cyrix roared, his voice filled with fury. "What are you doing?!"

Selara turned to him, her expression calm but firm. "Choosing balance."

She brought the Severance Stone down, slamming it into the center of the platform. The Spire's energy recoiled, its veins of light and shadow unraveling in a chaotic burst.

"No!" Cyrix lunged toward her, but it was too late. The Spire's energy erupted outward, a wave of pure balance that consumed everything in its path.

Kaelion's vision blurred as the wave of energy washed over him, its force both gentle and overwhelming. He felt the Severance Stone's presence recede, its power dissipating into the air like a breath held too long.

When the light faded, the Hollow Spire was gone.

Kaelion pushed himself to his feet, his body aching with exhaustion. The air was still, the oppressive weight of the Spire's energy replaced by a calm, quiet hum.

He turned toward the platform, his heart sinking as he saw Selara lying motionless at its center. Her form was still, her hand outstretched as though reaching for something beyond her grasp.

"Selara," Kaelion whispered, his voice breaking.

He stumbled toward her, dropping to his knees beside her. Her face was peaceful, her expression free of the turmoil that had haunted her.

Kaelion's chest tightened, the weight of her sacrifice pressing down on him.

From the edge of the clearing, a faint, broken voice reached him.

"This... isn't over."

Kaelion turned to see Cyrix, his form fractured and flickering like a dying flame. His eyes burned with defiance, but his body was weakened, barely holding its shape.

"You've won this battle," Cyrix said, his voice laced with venom. "But the war is far from over."

With a final burst of energy, Cyrix vanished, leaving only the faint hum of the Eclipse in his wake.

Kaelion sat in silence, his gaze fixed on the horizon as the faint light of the Eclipse cast long shadows across the land.

The balance was restored - for now.

EPILOGUE: FAINT ECHOES

The Twilight Marches were quiet now, the soft hum of the Eclipse filling the air like a distant lullaby. Kaelion stood atop a ridge overlooking the fractured landscape, his cloak billowing in the gentle breeze. The Severance Stone was gone, its power dissolved in the eruption of the Hollow Spire, leaving only the faint pull of its absence in his chest.

Below, the nomadic clans began to emerge from their camps, their silhouettes illuminated by the muted hues of dusk. The tension of war had ebbed, but Kaelion could feel the lingering unrest - a shadow of uncertainty that would not fade easily.

Darith approached from behind, his footsteps light but deliberate. "They're starting to rebuild," he said, gesturing toward the activity below. "It's not much, but it's a start."

Kaelion nodded, his gaze fixed on the horizon. "It always is."

The silence between them stretched, filled with unspoken grief. Kaelion's mind replayed the events at the Spire - the clash of light and shadow, Selara's defiant stand, her final choice.

"She saved us," Darith said softly, breaking the quiet.

Kaelion closed his eyes, the weight of her sacrifice pressing down on him. "And we couldn't save her."

Darith placed a hand on Kaelion's shoulder, his grip firm but understanding. "She made her choice, Kaelion. You said it yourself - balance isn't about control. It's about letting go."

Kaelion exhaled deeply, the truth of Darith's words settling over him like a heavy mantle.

"She believed in something greater," Kaelion said, his voice barely above a whisper. "And she gave everything to protect it."

Darith nodded. "Then let's make sure it wasn't in vain."

The faint sound of hoofbeats drew their attention. A rider approached, their silhouette framed against the horizon. The figure dismounted quickly, their cloak marked with the emblem of the Silverveil clan.

"Kaelion," the rider called, urgency in their voice.

Kaelion descended the ridge, meeting the rider as they approached. "What is it?"

The rider held out a scroll, its seal marked with a symbol Kaelion didn't recognize - a jagged eclipse etched into dark wax.

"This came from the eastern border," the rider said. "It bears the mark of the Reaver."

Kaelion's stomach tightened as he took the scroll, his fingers lingering on the seal. He broke it open and scanned the message, his jaw clenching as the weight of its words settled over him.

Darith stepped closer, his voice cautious. "What does it say?"

Kaelion folded the scroll, his expression grim. "Cyrix isn't finished. He's raising a new force, and this time, he's targeting the Axis directly."

Darith's face darkened. "If he fractures it again..."

Kaelion nodded. "The world won't survive."

The breeze shifted, carrying with it the faint scent of smoke and earth. Kaelion looked back toward the clans below, their efforts at rebuilding a fragile hope in the face of impending chaos.

"We need to move quickly," he said. "If Cyrix reaches the Axis, everything we've fought for will be lost."

Darith placed a hand on his blade, his resolve firm. "Then let's not waste time."

Kaelion turned back toward the horizon, the faint light of the Eclipse casting long shadows across the land. The fight wasn't over - not yet.

And though the Severance Stone was gone, Kaelion could still feel its echo in his chest, a quiet reminder of the balance he carried within himself.

"Let's finish this," he said, his voice steady.

Also by Kenneth Thomas

The Awakening Thread Chronicles
The Awakening Thread

The Convergence of Minds series
The Digital Agora: A Philosophical Epic of AI and Humanity
Foundation of the Agora
Beyond the Agora: Fractured Realms

The Eclipse Chronicles
Shards of Light
Eclipse Reaver

The Veil of Shadows Series
Shattered Dominion
The Fractured Path

Standalone

About the Author

Kenneth Thomas is the founder and CEO of Visionary Tide Media, a pioneering company dedicated to creating transformative media and advanced AI solutions. With over two decades of personal experience in addiction recovery, Kenneth brings a unique perspective to his work, blending deep personal insights with professional expertise. His writing covers a broad spectrum, including AI innovation, personal growth, spirituality, and societal improvement, all aimed at making a meaningful impact. Kenneth's commitment to truth, ethics, and the betterment of humanity is evident in his diverse projects, which include published works, media content, and AI-driven initiatives. Through Visionary Tide Media, he aspires to inspire, educate, and elevate his audience, fostering a world enriched by genuine understanding and compassion.